PUFFIN BOOKS

# SUPERPOWERS
## THE SNARLING BEAST

Books by Alex Cliff
SUPERPOWERS series

# SUPER
## THE SNARLING BEAST
# POWERS

**ALEX CLIFF**

ILLUSTRATED BY LEO HARTAS

PUFFIN

PUFFIN BOOKS

Published by the Penguin Group
Penguin Books Ltd, 80 Strand, London WC2R ORL, England
Penguin Group (USA) Inc., 375 Hudson Street, New York, New York 10014, USA
Penguin Group (Canada), 90 Eglinton Avenue East, Suite 700, Toronto, Ontario, Canada M4P 2Y3
(a division of Pearson Penguin Canada Inc.)
Penguin Ireland, 25 St Stephen's Green, Dublin 2, Ireland (a division of Penguin Books Ltd)
Penguin Group (Australia), 250 Camberwell Road, Camberwell, Victoria 3124, Australia
(a division of Pearson Australia Group Pty Ltd)
Penguin Books India Pvt Ltd, 11 Community Centre, Panchsheel Park,
New Delhi – 110 017, India
Penguin Group (NZ), 67 Apollo Drive, Rosedale, North Shore 0632, New Zealand
(a division of Pearson New Zealand Ltd)
Penguin Books (South Africa) (Pty) Ltd, 24 Sturdee Avenue, Rosebank,
Johannesburg 2196, South Africa

Penguin Books Ltd, Registered Offices: 80 Strand, London WC2R ORL, England

puffinbooks.com

Published 2007
1

Text copyright © Alex Cliff, 2007
Illustrations copyright © Leo Hartas, 2007
All rights reserved

The moral right of the author and illustrator has been asserted

Set in Bembo
Typeset by Palimpsest Book Production Limited, Grangemouth, Stirlingshire
Made and printed in England by Clays Ltd, St Ives plc

British Library Cataloguing in Publication Data
A CIP catalogue record for this book is available from the British Library

ISBN: 978-0-141-32138-7

# CONTENTS

# JUST IMAGINE . . .

a hawk swooping towards a ruined
castle on a hill. With a savage scream,
the bird flies into the castle keep. As it
lands beside the one tower that is still
standing, its body starts to stretch and
grow. Within seconds it has become a
woman. She is twice as tall as an
ordinary woman and a cloak of
brown-grey feathers swirls from her

shoulders. Her black eyes flash with angry fire.

She claps her hands together and a square of stones on the inner wall of the tower crumbles.

As the dust clears, a tall man with long hair and a noble face looks out

through the gap. He is trapped inside the tower's thick walls. This is the superhero Hercules. He meets the evil goddess's angry gaze without flinching. 'Another day dawns, Juno,' he says. 'By the end of today I will have my sixth superpower back.'

'No!' Juno hisses.

'Yes,' Hercules snaps back. 'For five days now you have set the two human boys a task to do each day. Each day they have won a superpower back for me. Soon I will have all my powers back and you will not be able to keep me as your prisoner any longer. I will break free from these walls!' He thumps the inside of the tower with both fists.

'Never!' Juno exclaims. 'I will kill the boys first.'

'You cannot!' Hercules' voice raps out.
'You made a deal with them, Juno. The
boys are allowed to choose one of my
superpowers each day to help them
complete a task you set. If they succeed
the superpower returns to me. You
know as well as I, that although the

4

boys can be hurt or killed while carrying out the task, you must *not* injure them directly. You cannot break the rules, Juno. Gods play fair when they deal with humans.'

'You dare to tell *me* what gods do?' Juno cries in outrage.

'Yes,' Hercules declares.

They stare at each other, superhero and evil goddess. They have been enemies for centuries.

'It is true!' Juno spits. 'I might not be able to kill the boys myself while we have a deal, but I can make the task they have to complete as dangerous as I like.' Her eyes light up suddenly. '*Doubly* dangerous in fact.'

Hercules frowns. 'What do you mean?'

'You'll find out soon enough!' Juno's

cruel mouth curves into a smile. 'And so will they!' She claps her hands. There is a crash of thunder and the stones re-form over Hercules, trapping him once again in his magical prison. 'Who's powerless now, Hercules?' Juno breathes. A flash of lightning strikes down. As it hits the ground, the goddess transforms into a hawk again.

Beating her powerful wings, she speeds away across the dawn-streaked sky.

# CHAPTER ONE

## STONE, PAPER, SCISSORS

Max Hayward and Finlay Yates were facing each other in the lounge in Max's house. Their hands were balled into fists.

'After three,' Max said, looking at Finlay.

Finlay nodded.

Max counted them in. 'One, two . . . *three!*'

Their fists moved lightning fast and they shouted at the same time.

'Scissors!' said Finlay, his fingers making a scissors shape.

'Paper!' said Max, his hand flattening.

'I win!' Finlay exclaimed triumphantly. 'Scissors cut paper. Let's do it again. One, two . . . *three!*'

'Scissors!' he shouted.

'Stone!' Max shouted at the same time, keeping his fingers curled into a ball. 'I win! Stone blunts scissors!'

'Best of three?' Finlay suggested.

Max nodded. This time Finlay called out 'paper' and Max went for stone again.

'I win this time,' Finlay said. 'Paper wraps stone.' He grabbed Max's hand, and made his voice sound all creepy. 'I am the evil hand of paper. I will destroy you!' He changed to a dalek's voice

8

from *Doctor Who*. 'I will exterminate!'
He grabbed Max round the neck.

Max ducked and grabbed Finlay's legs
behind the knees.

'Oof!' Finlay exclaimed as he lost his
balance. He yanked Max's ankles as he
fell, and Max crashed down with him.
They wrestled for a moment and then
Finlay suddenly pulled away, his thick
blonde hair sticking up.

'Hey, I've had an idea! Let's change
the game. How about cannonball, sword
and net instead of stone, scissors, paper?'

Max realized what he was getting at.
'Yeah! So a sword could cut a net but
be blown up by a cannonball?' he said.

Finlay nodded. 'And a net could catch
a cannonball. What d'you reckon?'

'It's cool!' Max replied. 'Better than

the real game. I've never got that bit about paper beating stone by wrapping round it, but a net *could* actually catch a cannonball. What hand shapes should we use?'

They were just working them out, when Max's dad came into the room. 'Hi, you two. Got any plans for today?'

'We're going to the castle again,' Max replied, glancing at the clock above the mantelpiece. It was eight-thirty. 'We should go soon,' he said to Finlay.

'You've been at the castle every day this half-term,' Mr Hayward said curiously. 'What are you doing there?'

Finlay wondered what Mr Hayward would say if they told him the truth – that they were helping the superhero Hercules escape from his castle prison.

'Just stuff,' Max replied vaguely.

'Oh, well, so long as you're having fun and not getting into any trouble,' said Mr Hayward.

'Oh, no trouble, Dad,' Max answered quickly.

*Not much*, Finlay thought, picturing the Man-Eating Birds they had killed the day before. Max still had a wound on his arm from where one of the birds had slashed at him with its razor-sharp beak. Every day, either Finlay or Max seemed to end up with a scar from facing Juno's challenges.

'Have I told you that the castle used to be a Roman temple for the goddess Juno,' Mr Hayward said to Finlay.

Finlay nodded. *About twenty million times*, he thought to himself. Max's dad was really into history and was always talking about it.

'Max and I have been reading some of the Roman myths and legends together,' Mr Hayward went on. 'I'm sure you'd like them too, Fin. They're fascinating.'

'Yeah,' Finlay said politely. He hastily grabbed Max's arm before Mr Hayward could start telling him one of the stories. 'Let's go, Max!'

'See you later, Dad,' Max called.

'If we survive today,' muttered Finlay as they hurried out of the lounge.

Five minutes later Max and Finlay were running up the path that led from the village to the castle. The castle's crumbling walls formed a circle around a grassy keep. On the outside of the walls was a dark moat. The boys crossed the stone bridge and scrambled through the gatehouse – the entrance to the castle. The tower in which Hercules was imprisoned was opposite them. Its grey stones stood in shadow.

'We're early,' Finlay said to Max.

Every morning, just as the sun's rays fell on the gatehouse wall, the stones in front of Hercules' face crumbled so that he could see out. At the same time, his superpowers, which Juno had placed in the gatehouse archway, glowed brightly.

'It's almost time,' Max said.

As he spoke, there was a crash of thunder overhead and a bolt of lightning shot down from the sky. The boys blinked as Juno appeared in front of them.

'Maggots!' Juno snapped, glaring at the boys. 'Worms!'

Finlay and Max hastily backed away. They were used to being called names by Juno now and knew it was better not to object.

*Not unless you wanted to be frozen in*

*mid-air, unable to move or speak*, Max thought nervously as the goddess stared at them.

'Today is your sixth task,' she said. 'You must find and return my three golden apples. They are hidden nearby.' Her black eyes narrowed. 'Or, of course, you could just give up now because you will *never* succeed.'

'We won't give up!' Finlay said strongly.

'No way. Where do we have to look for these apples?' Max said. As he met Juno's terrible gaze, he felt his stomach plunge downwards as if he was in a very fast lift.

'I have placed the apples in the grounds of the Manor House in your village,' she replied sharply. 'Look for them in the walled garden with the statue of Cerberus in the centre.'

'Ceber-what?' Finlay echoed.

'It's a mythical beast,' Max muttered to him. 'A three-headed dog. Dad and I've been reading about it.' He looked at Juno. He knew how tricky she could be and he wanted to make sure they'd got the task straight. 'So all we've got to do is find these apples and bring them back here?'

Juno smiled dangerously. 'Yes. That is *all* you have to do. Though of course,' she added, 'first you must choose the correct three apples.'

Max felt alarmed. 'How many are there?' he asked, imagining hundreds of apples to choose from.

'Just four,' Juno replied. 'But choose

wrong and you will *not* live to regret it.'
She gave a delighted laugh.

Finlay and Max exchanged worried
looks.

'So how will we know which are the
*right* apples?' Finlay said. 'Or do we just
have to guess?'

'That would be *much* more fun,'
Juno said. 'But no, I must give you a
fair chance, and so I will give you
a riddle that will tell you which apple
to leave – if you can solve it.' Juno
clicked her fingers and a piece of
folded paper instantly appeared in her
hand. It was sealed with a circle of
blood-red wax. She held it out to
Finlay. 'Here!'

She looked down her nose at them
both. 'I don't imagine either of you

will be able to solve it. It takes wit
and wisdom to find answers in a riddle.
You will fail in your task this time. Wait
and see!'

She clapped her hands. There was
another flash of lightning and a hawk
soared upwards out of the keep.

# CHAPTER TWO

## WHICH SUPERPOWER?

'So we've got to solve a riddle,' Max said, looking excitedly at the folded piece of paper. He liked riddles and word puzzles.

'Yeah,' said Finlay, sounding doubtful. He didn't.

'Let's open it!' said Max, but just then the sun rose a fraction higher in the sky. There was the sound of crumbling and grinding and a rectangle of stones on the inner tower wall crumbled away.

Hercules looked out. 'Boys!'

'Hello, Hercules,' Max said eagerly. 'We've just seen Juno. We've got to bring back three golden apples from a garden . . .'

'Making sure we choose the right three,' Finlay put in.

'And we've got a riddle to help us,' Max added. 'There are only four apples. It doesn't seem a very difficult task.'

'Do not underestimate Juno,' Hercules warned. 'She is angry and I am worried about what she has planned today. You *must* be careful.'

'We will be,' Max promised.

Finlay looked round at the gatehouse. There were eight stones around its arched entrance. Two of the stones were now glowing with magic symbols, their images carved in lines of burning white fire. Both those two stones held a superpower. Once there had been seven superpowers glowing in the stones but every time the boys took one to try and return it to Hercules, its symbol disappeared from the wall.

*Today I get to choose another*, Finlay thought, looking at the two symbols that were left. There was a lion to represent courage and a stag leaping to represent super-agility. 'I'd better get our superpower for the day,' he said, shoving the riddle into his pocket.

'And which will you choose?' asked Hercules.

Finlay looked at the lion and the stag.

Agility meant being brilliant at jumping and climbing and leaping, which would be a cool power to have. Being courageous didn't sound nearly so much fun. But maybe they'd need the power of agility the next day. Stealing three golden apples didn't seem difficult, but then again, if he had to make a life or death choice over which apples to take maybe he might need some extra courage . . .

Finlay felt torn. Should he choose the power he wanted or should he be sensible and think of the tasks ahead? It was a difficult decision to make. He remembered a time when he had faced the same choice and made the wrong decision.

'I'll choose courage,' he decided. Max grinned at him.

However, Hercules looked uncertain. 'It is a tricky power to have,' he said slowly. 'You have already proved yourself to be extremely courageous over the last five days. Beware of false courage; it can cloud your judgement.'

'So should I choose agility instead?' Finlay asked in surprise.

Hercules frowned. 'No. I do not think so. That power will certainly be of more use tomorrow.'

'Courage it is, then!' Finlay said. 'I'm going to get it!' He ran across the grass and, stopping in front of the archway, he put his hand firmly on to the stone with the lion symbol. For a moment Finlay felt the shape burning into the palm of his hand and then heat started flowing down his arm. It tingled all the way through his body down to his feet.

At last the stone felt cold beneath Finlay's fingers. He took a deep breath. He was filled with a warm glow. He felt amazing, like he could do anything. There was nothing and no one that could stand in his way. He almost wished the sabre-toothed lion they'd fought in the first task was standing in front of him. He'd fight it single-handedly! And as for the Nine-Headed River Monster . . . He swung round to Max. 'What are we waiting for? Let's go and get those apples!'

'Hang on! Shouldn't we open the riddle and show it to Hercules first?' Max protested. 'He might be able to help us figure out its meaning.'

'We'll be fine!' Finlay declared and he ran out through the gatehouse archway.

Max glanced at Hercules, not sure what to do.

'Go with him,' Hercules said quickly.

'The new courage added to his own not inconsiderable bravery might make him act foolishly. He has the riddle. It will contain the answers you need. Use it wisely. Remember, even if all seems lost there will always be a way out if you look hard enough. There is always a fair chance. That is the rule of the gods when they deal with humans. Go on now! Go!' he urged.

Max charged after Finlay, his heart pounding. What exactly *did* Juno have in store for them that day?

# CHAPTER THREE

## KEEP OUT!

The Manor House was in the centre of the village. It was a very large, old house with big gardens, a tennis court and tall black gates.

'How are we going to get into the grounds?' Max said as he caught up with Finlay. 'The gates are always locked.'

'We climb over the gate of course,' Finlay said as if it were obvious.

Max stared at him. 'But they're enormous and there are spikes on top! And what about if someone sees us and . . .'

'We'll be fine!' said Finlay, as if deadly spikes were no problem at all.

Max hurried after him, feeling very worried by Finlay's courageous words. He was sure they wouldn't be fine if they tried to climb over the gates!

However, when they got to the Manor House they found that they were in luck. The gates were open and there was a big sign on them saying: '*Brownies Half-Term Music and Craft Day on the Tennis Courts. This way*'. An arrow pointed down a path that led through some trees into the gardens.

'Come on!' Finlay said, marching

through the gates and taking the path
the arrow pointed to.

'Fin!' Max exclaimed. 'We can't just
walk in.'

'Why not?' Finlay said, striding on
down the path.

Max ran after him. 'What if someone sees us?'

'So what? I'm not scared! We just tell them we're looking for three golden apples,' Finlay replied.

Max dragged him off the path, pulling him behind a nearby bush. 'Are you mad? We can't say stuff like that! We have to be careful.' He glanced round. 'Look, if this Brownies' thing is this way, towards the tennis courts, why don't we check out the grounds at the back of the house? There'll be less people to spot us there.'

Finlay shrugged. 'One way's as good as the other, I guess!' He turned and marched in the opposite direction.

Max hastened after him, his heart

sinking. Maybe Hercules was right. Maybe Finlay having extra courage wasn't such a good idea!

The Manor House was in the middle of being repaired. It was covered in scaffolding and was separated from the garden by yellow plastic tape with '*Unsafe, Keep Out*' written all along it.

Finlay ducked underneath the tape. Max checked that no one was watching and quickly followed him.

They hurried round the back of the house. The gardens here were completely deserted. The only sounds to break the silence were the chirrup of birds and the faint sound of musical instruments floating on the breeze from the direction of the tennis courts.

As Finlay and Max reached the back
of the house, they saw a separate walled
garden. There was a moss-covered
archway that led into it. Just through
the entrance was a basin of water
supporting a tall stone pillar with a

bronze statue of a cherub standing on top — a fountain. The cherub was facing into the garden and blowing out through a trumpet.

'Is that the cere-thingy that Juno was talking about?' asked Finlay, going over to the cherub.

Max looked at the podgy baby with wings. 'Does that look like a three-headed dog to you?'

'Hmmm. Guess not.' Finlay walked past the cherub and into the garden. On the left-hand side the walls were crumbling, while on the other three sides the walls were fully repaired, high and sheer. Around the fountain the ground was covered with gravel, but in the centre of the garden was a large square of grass.

'Hey! Now that's more like it!' Finlay exclaimed, pointing at a dramatic stone statue on the grass. It was a statue of the most terrifying creature that Max had ever seen and that included river monsters, giant boars and sabre-toothed lions!

'Cool!' said Finlay, going over to investigate the gigantic three-headed beast. Its stone coat was carved to look wild and matted; it had a huge, scaly dragon's tail and its enormous dog paws had long, sharp nails that stretched out at wicked angles. But most terrifying of all were its heads. The first head was lowered almost to the ground. It looked to the side with an expression of pure evil. Its lip curled, and its eyes seemed to scour the courtyard, looking for

something to devour. The second head
was pointing straight up, clearly howling
like a werewolf baying at the moon.
The third head was stretching out of
the courtyard, towards the rest of the
gardens. Every tooth was clearly visible,
gleaming in a wide death-bite that
looked as if it could crush a person
in an instant.

Max shivered and looked away,
having to remind himself that it was
just a statue. At the far end of the
walled garden, behind the grassy
square, was a shed with double doors
that were wide open. He stared. At the
back of the shed was a long stone
bench, and arranged along it were four
small stone pedestals, each topped with
a shining golden apple. He could

hardy believe his eyes. 'Finlay! Look, there are the apples!' he exclaimed, pointing at the shed. 'We've found them already!'

'This has to be the easiest task ever,' Fin said in delight. 'Come on, let's go and get the three we need!'

Finlay left the statue and hurried on to the flagstoned path that led around the grassy square to the shed. But as his foot touched the third flagstone, the ground beneath him seemed to drop a bit, there was a grinding noise and before Finlay knew what was happening he and Max were being soaked with water.

'What's going on?' spluttered Finlay.

'It's coming from the cherub!' Max gasped.

A jet of water was flying out of the cherub's trumpet straight up into the air. It rained down from the sky, drenching the two boys and everything around them – the flagstones, the grass and the stone statue . . .

'It's a trick fountain!' Finlay exclaimed, jumping off the stone and pulling Max with him. 'We must have started it off by treading on this flagstone!' As they jumped off the flagstone the fountain stopped. The last few water droplets rained down around them.

Suddenly there was the violent sound of stone breaking.

They swung round.

A spiderweb of cracks had begun to run down the stone statue of Cerberus from its three heads to its great clawed feet.

Max and Finlay gasped as matted grey fur began to burst through the splits in the stone.

'It's coming to life!' Fin yelled.

As he spoke, all three of the beast's heads moved; the stone crumbling away to reveal yellow teeth, slavering jaws and burning coal-black eyes that fixed on the boys like lasers. The monster took a pace towards them, all its heads growling together.

'Let's get out of here!' Max shouted.

He began to run. It took him a few seconds to realize that Finlay wasn't with him. Max swung round. To his horror, Finlay was still standing by the grassy square, facing up to the three-headed mutant dog. 'You wanna fight? I'll give you a fight!' he was shouting. 'You're nothing but an overgrown puppy!'

'Fin!' Max yelled in horror.

*Keep Out!*

The dog paused for a second,
streaming thick drool from its savage
jaws. Then it crouched low and
prepared to spring . . .

# CHAPTER FOUR

## TOMB RAIDER!

Max didn't stop to think twice. Racing to the square, he grabbed Finlay and yanked him away just as the monster sprang. It landed right where Finlay had been standing. Finlay yelled and struggled but Max didn't give up. He dragged Finlay backwards towards the fountain. The dog threw back its heads and howled. Max saw its razor-sharp teeth and fear ran like ice down his spine. That thing was going to get them! This was it! This was the end!

He shut his eyes as the dog leapt forwards, expecting to feel teeth tearing into his flesh at any moment.

*Clank!* The metallic sound was followed by a snarl of frustration.

Max's eyes flew open. The dog had been pulled up short by the chains round its necks. It bayed in rage. The chains rattled and clanked, attached to huge metal rings set into the statue's plinth. They creaked ominously, but for now they held firm.

'Let me go! I'll get it! Just let me at it!' Fin shouted, struggling to get free.

'Stop it, Finlay!' Max exclaimed. 'Who d'you think you are? Scrappy Doo?

That thing's much too big for you to fight!'

But Finlay continued to struggle. 'Let me at it!'

Seeing an empty plant pot standing near the fountain, Max let go of Finlay

with one arm, picked up the pot, swished it through the water in the stone dish under the fountain and emptied it straight over Finlay's head.

'W-what are you doing?' Finlay spluttered as the water dripped down his face.

Cerberus barked and growled as he strained at his metal chains, his dragon's tail thrashing from side to side, the cruel spikes along his back bristling.

Max grabbed Finlay's shoulders and looked him in the face. 'You're mental, Finlay. You can't fight that thing. Not without weapons or super-strength or something. It'll eat you!'

Finlay hesitated and then wiped his face on his T-shirt. 'You might be right,' he admitted. The shock of the water seemed to have calmed him down slightly. 'It *is* really big.'

'It's huge!' Max said, above the sound of the dog's ferocious growling. A thought suddenly struck him. 'And anyway we don't need to fight it. That's not part of the task, we just need to get round it to get to the apples.'

Finlay frowned. 'Yeah, I suppose Juno never actually said we had to fight it.'

Max glanced at the straining chains. They were quite rusty. How much longer would they stand up to Cerberus throwing himself about? And if the monster broke free it wasn't just him and Finlay it might attack. What about the Brownies on the tennis courts or what about if it went into the village? Max gulped. They had to get the apples and get back to the castle. The sooner they completed the task, the sooner Cerberus would turn back to stone and everyone would be safe.

'We need to get round it somehow,' he said quickly. Cerberus could reach all the way to the walls at the left and right of the garden, although the chains were too short for him to reach the shed or to the fountain by the entrance. 'There's no way we'll be able to run past it; it'll get us in an instant. Maybe we should try and distract it or something . . .' Max broke off, an idea suddenly tugging at the back of his mind. He knew something about Cerberus. As he tried to remember the stories he'd read with his dad, he suddenly realized that Finlay was

heading towards the crumbling
left-hand wall.

'Fin, what are you doing?' Max asked.
'Where are you going?'

Finlay swung round. 'We might not

be able to run past it on the ground but we can if we go along that wall!' he exclaimed. 'I'm going to climb up on top of it, run along and get to the shed at the back of the garden.'

'You can't do that!' Max looked at the disintegrating wall. 'It's much too dangerous!'

'I'll be OK,' Finlay said confidently. 'It'll be like being in *Tomb Raider*!'

'*Tomb Raider!*' Max echoed, thinking of the computer game he had at home. 'But you're not Lara Croft, Fin! And you haven't got unlimited lives. You've only got one!'

'One life's all I need!' Finlay grinned and he set off at a run, leaping over the fourth flagstone in a single bound.

'Fin! Come back!' Max yelled. But

Finlay was sprinting towards the wall.

With a horrible howl, the dog
bounded towards him, all six eyes
narrowed, three muzzles foaming
with spit. Just in time, Finlay found his
first foothold and propelled himself up
the wall. The dog's snapping teeth
missed his ankle by millimetres, and
before it could try again Finlay started
scaling the stone, digging his fingertips
into the tiniest cracks in the mortar and
grabbing sticking-out bricks without a
moment's thought. His fingers caught
the top of the wall and he heaved
himself up into a crouching position.

But Cerberus wasn't about to give up.
The beast got ready to spring.

'Watch your legs, Finlay!' Max yelled.
Finlay straightened up. 'Come on,

then, Fido!' he yelled down to it. 'Catch me if you can!'

Muscles rippled in the beast's legs as it leapt up towards the top of the wall. To Max's horror, Finlay started clowning around, balancing on one leg as three sets of jaws hurtled up towards him, ready to tear him to pieces. But with centimetres to spare before it crushed him, Cerberus was stopped short by his chains. His heads snapped back, jaws clapping shut again, and he fell back, furious.

'Yay! Look at me!' Finlay called, waving at Max. But as he did so, a loose stone started to give way under his feet. Max caught his breath, but Finlay just leapt forward bravely on to a more secure piece of wall. 'Here I go – check *this* out!'

He began running along the top of the wall.

Barking furiously, Cerberus bounded alongside him. Finlay just kept on running. Reaching a piece where the

wall had crumbled almost completely away he leapt into the air.

'Finlay!' Max yelled.

But Finlay managed to land on the other side of the gap. 'Whoa!' he gasped, almost falling but just managing to stop himself.

Cerberus howled in frustration and leapt again. The chains clanked and the metal rings in the ground creaked as the dog threw its immense body weight forward.

'Can't get me!' Finlay taunted it, continuing along the wall. When he was almost at the end of the garden, Finlay turned round and yelled at Max, 'How cool am I?'

But he spoke too soon. As the words left his mouth, the brickwork beneath him suddenly collapsed.

'Argh!' Finlay yelled. His arms windmilled wildly as he began to fall.

Howling with triumph, gnashing his yellow, foam-flecked teeth, Cerberus lunged towards him, ready for the kill . . .

# CHAPTER FIVE

## MAX'S PLAN

As Finlay fell he grabbed the top of the
remaining wall with his hands. He
hung on by his fingertips. For a
moment, Max thought Finlay was
going to lose his grip and slip straight
into the dog's open jaws but then with
a tremendous kick, Finlay managed to
get his chest up on to the wall. He
threw his leg over the stones and

pulled himself up just as the dog sprang.

'Hey!' he called cheerfully to Max, as Cerberus fell back with a frustrated howl. 'That was close!'

Max's heart was pounding. 'You're crazy!'

'Don't worry,' Finlay said, jumping into a crouch and then standing up. 'I'm almost there.' He ran along the last bit of wall and leapt down just out of Cerberus's reach.

Cerberus ran to the end of his chains, barking savagely.

'Aw, poor little doggy,' Finlay teased it. 'Now for the apples!' he called to Max. 'The sooner I get back with them the better.'

'But how are you going to get back

now the wall's fallen down?' Max
pointed out, looking at the huge gap in
the wall. It looked like a giant had
taken a massive bite out of the top of it

– leaving behind a ragged gap easily four metres across. 'You can't jump that, and if you climb down, Cerberus will eat you!'

Finlay looked and, for a moment, doubt flickered through his eyes. But then he lifted his chin. 'I can try to jump it,' he called back bravely.

'It's much too far!' Max exclaimed. His mind raced. 'We'll have to distract Cerberus, so you can get past him or something . . .' Suddenly the thought that had been bugging Max exploded into his mind. 'Of course!' he exclaimed. 'I remember now. In the story about Cerberus, Orpheus had to get past him and to do it he put him to sleep by playing music. Why don't we –'

'Later, Max,' Finlay interrupted impatiently. 'I'm going to get those apples!'

'But, Fin . . .' However, Finlay was already charging towards the shed at the back of the garden. Max hesitated for a moment and then turned and ran out of the walled garden, heading for the tennis courts.

Finlay ran to the workbench where the four golden apples were waiting. They glittered brightly. As he reached them he saw that each had a picture carved into its shining golden surface. The first apple had a picture of the wind blowing from a cloud, the second had a stream of water, the third had a flame and the fourth had a picture of a stone.

'Air, water, fire and earth,' Finlay muttered, looking at the symbols on the apples. 'And we have to choose one to leave. But which one?' He pulled the

paper with the riddle on out of his
pocket, ripped it open and read it out
loud:

'*Air and water, fire and earth*
*Were present at the goddess birth.*
*Three must you choose but take good care;*
*Choose wrong and you'll face deep despair.*
*All four are strong, one stands alone,*
*Fire dries water, which wears out stone,*
*Which comes from earth, which smothers air.*
*The answer's in the grassy square.*
*If you choose wrongly, mark these words:*
*Two elements may break a third.*
*The water from the cherub's breath*
*Can split the stone and save from death.*
*Superhero, do you now dare*
*Choose water, fire, earth or air?*'

Finlay felt a wave of confusion. What did it mean? He could see that there was one apple for air, one for earth, one for water and one for fire. He had to leave one apple and take the other three. But how did he know which was the wrong apple?

*Choose wrong and you'll face deep despair . . .*

He didn't like the sound of that at all!

He read through the riddle again. All the stuff about water, fire, earth and air. What was it going on about?

'Come on,' he muttered in frustration to himself. 'You can work this out!' But though he read it through several more times, it was no use. He couldn't find any answers in the riddle at all.

*I need Max*, he thought. *He's good at this sort of stuff!*

He hurried to the door of the shed.

'Max!' he shouted.

The three-headed monster lunged at him, long ribbons of drool dripping

from its teeth. Finlay jumped out of its way.

'Max!' he yelled again. But the courtyard was empty. He looked all about him in astonishment. Max had gone!

*Almost there*, Max thought as he crawled commando-style through the rhododendron bushes. He was nearly at the edge of the grass tennis courts where the Brownies were having their music and craft day.

His plan buzzed through his head. In the story he'd read with his dad, Orpheus, a kind of superhero, had managed to put Cerberus to sleep by playing a harp to him. Maybe he and Finlay could do the same. They didn't

have a harp. But maybe any musical
instrument would do.

*The Brownies must have lots of
instruments if they're having a music day!*
Max thought. Reaching the edge of the
bushes, he peered out.

On the far side of the tennis courts, a group of girls dressed in brown and yellow uniforms were painting pictures. Nearer to Max, a second group of girls were playing music with a jolly-looking woman.

There was a large plastic crate labelled *Instruments* just near the edge of the courts. Max could see a recorder, a drum and a small electronic keyboard sticking out of the top. His heart leapt. If he could just get one of those . . .

He eyed up the distance from the bushes to the box. It was about three metres. *I could probably get there and back without anyone noticing,* he thought.

*Of course it is stealing,* a voice in his head said.

Max ignored the voice. It wasn't *really* stealing, he told himself. Just borrowing. He'd bring the instrument back.

He was just about to make a dash for it when one of the girls in the group with the musical instruments put up her hand. 'Brown Owl, my keyboard's making a bit of a strange noise.'

'It's probably just the batteries running out,' the jolly-looking woman said. 'There's a spare keyboard in the instrument box. Go and fetch it and leave that one on the ground beside the box so no one else uses it.'

The girl ran over. When she stopped by the crate, she was only a few metres away from Max. He stayed as still as he could, hardly daring to breathe. What if she looked into the bush and saw him?

But to his relief the girl simply threw down the old keyboard, grabbed the spare one and hurried back to join the others.

Max checked the tennis courts. No one was watching. He crawled out from the bushes, ran with his head ducked as fast as he could, grabbed the old keyboard from the ground and dived back into the bushes. All the time he expected to hear a yell as someone noticed him. But no one called out, no one shouted. He'd got away with it! His heart banged against his ribs as he lay among the leaves, clutching the keyboard to his chest. He hadn't been seen!

Turning the volume down very low he pressed his ear to the speakers and pushed the play button on the keyboard. The backing track was set to 'Slow Ballad', and it sounded a bit wobbly and dragging. The woman called Brown Owl was right, the batteries were wearing out, but even though it sounded a bit odd, it was still music. Maybe it would work!

*I hope so*, Max prayed, and, switching the keyboard off, he set off back in the direction of the walled garden.

'Max!' Finlay yelled above the howling of the three-headed dog. 'Where've you gone?'

Max came running into the walled

garden. Twigs and leaves were sticking
out of his hair.

'Where have you been?' Finlay shouted
across the courtyard. 'I need you to help
me with this riddle. What's that?' he
exclaimed, seeing Max at the bottom of
the garden, the keyboard in his arms.

'Keyboard!' Max panted, his breath
coming in short gasps. 'To put Cerberus
to sleep. Orpheus did the same thing in
the underworld.'

Finlay looked at him in confusion.
'Who? Where? What?'

'Watch!' Max called. Switching the
keyboard on, he set it to 'Lullaby'
and turned the volume up full. Soft,
gentle music started playing. It burbled
a bit because of the batteries running
out but it still sounded quite restful.

Holding his breath, Max looked at
the dog. 'If he's like the Cerberus in the
stories, it should make him feel sleepy,'

he called to Finlay as quietly as he could. All three of the dog's heads looked towards him. Suddenly it sat down and yawned.

'Do you think it's working?' Finlay hissed in amazement.

Max stared. Surely it couldn't be this easy?

But it did seem to be.

The dog yawned again and then lay down. With a swish of its dragon's tail, it laid its heads between its great taloned paws and then shut all six of its eyes.

Within a minute it was breathing heavily. Max looked across the grass at Finlay. 'Should I try getting past it?' he hissed.

Finlay nodded eagerly. 'Quick,

before those batteries run out completely!'

Max stepped forward. The dog lifted one of its heads. Max froze. But the dog was only shifting its position slightly. Giving a loud snore, it settled down peacefully on its side.

'Come on!' whispered Finlay urgently.

Heart beating fast, Max began to tiptoe closer . . .

# CHAPTER SIX

## RISKING THE RIDDLE

Max could see the dog's sharp yellow teeth and its three lolling tongues. He crept past the first head, past the second, past the . . .

*Thud!* His foot kicked a stone on the ground. Max froze, almost too scared to look to see if Cerberus had awoken.

But the beast slept on.

Max hesitated and then ran the last

bit as fast as he could. He reached
Finlay, his breath coming in short gasps.

'That was such a cool idea to use the
music!' Finlay whispered as Max
reached him.

'Thanks,' Max panted back. 'Come on.
Let's get the apples and get out of here
before it wakes up!'

They ran into the shed together. The
four golden apples glowed at them, all
identical apart from the pictures
engraved into their sides.

'I just don't know which three to
choose,' said Finlay, going over to the
bench. He pulled the riddle out of his
pocket. 'And this doesn't help at all.'

'Give it here.' Max took it from him
and read quickly through it. 'So we've
got four apples.' He studied the apples.

'One is earth, one is fire, one is water and one is air.'

'Yeah, I got that far,' Finlay said. 'But which do we leave?'

Max read out:

*'All four are strong, one stands alone.*
*Fire dries water, which wears out stone,*
*Which comes from earth, which smothers air,*
*The answer's in the grassy square.'*

He paused for a moment. 'It's almost like it's talking about which of the elements is the strongest,' he said slowly. 'Like when we play paper, scissors and stone.'

Finlay's eyes widened. 'Do you think we have to work out which is the strongest element and leave that one alone?' He looked at the riddle. 'Well, in that case, the answer's obvious, isn't it? Fire's got to be the strongest. Air's the weakest because it can be smothered by earth, but then earth, when it's stone, can be worn away by water. The only thing that can beat water is fire. It says here, "*Fire dries water*"!' He looked very excited. 'We've got it, Max! I bet we have to leave the apple with the fire picture on. Come on, let's take the other three and get out of here!'

'Wait!' Max exclaimed, but Finlay was already grabbing the two apples with the water and wind symbols.

Max gasped, but nothing happened.

'These two are OK, then!' Finlay grinned. 'I am *so* right about this riddle! We just need to take the earth one and we're done.' He shoved the two apples he'd taken into his pockets and reached out to pick up the one with the picture of a stone on, but Max gripped his arm.

'No,' he said urgently. 'I'm not sure we've got the riddle right. If it is like stone, paper, scissors, then there isn't a winner. There's always one that can beat the other. There isn't one that's the strongest. I think it's a red herring . . .'

'A red herring!' Finlay looked astonished. 'What's a fish got to do with it?'

Max sighed. 'A red herring's a name for a false clue. Riddles often have them. I think this riddle's tricking us, by making us think we have to work out which is the strongest, but actually there isn't an answer to that question. After all, if you think about it, water can put out fire, can't it? I think the answer to which apple to leave is somewhere else in the riddle. Look at the fifth line: "*one stands alone*". I bet that's a big clue. And look,' he pointed at the eighth line. 'It says, "*The answer's in the grassy square.*" '

They looked outside at the square of grass. The dog was still asleep. 'Maybe you're right,' Finlay said uncertainly. 'Well, there's air in the square, because there's air everywhere. And there's water from the fountain. There isn't fire or stone. Though . . .' He frowned thoughtfully. 'There *was* stone when the dog was a statue. So, the only thing that isn't there is fire! Fire *has* to be the answer to the riddle!'

'No, hang on. If fire's not in the square, it *can't* be right!' Max protested.

'I reckon that bit of the riddle just doesn't make sense,' said Finlay impatiently. 'Let's ignore it.'

'You can't just ignore a bit of a riddle,' Max argued. 'Riddles don't work like that. Look, we have to think this through. We have to be logical . . .'

'Pants to logic!' Finlay said. 'It's fire, Max!' He lunged forward. Max tried to grab his arm to stop him but this time he was too late. Finlay's fingers closed around the apple with the stone symbol.

*Crack!* There was a loud snapping noise.

'What's that?' Max gasped as Finlay charged out into the courtyard with the apple.

'My hands!' yelled Finlay, stopping dead.

Max stared. The apple was still golden but Finlay's fingers were turning grey – grey and hard like stone.

'Fin!' Max gasped as the grey stone spread up Finlay's arms and down over his body.

Finlay tried to move towards him but he couldn't move. He looked at Max with horrified eyes. 'I'm . . .' His voice choked and stopped as his head turned grey.

He had turned to stone!

# CHAPTER SEVEN

## THE CHERUB'S TRUMPET

'No!' Max yelled. Finlay stood in front of him like a stone statue. The golden apple glittered evilly in his hands.

A great wave of sickness welled up inside Max. Finlay couldn't be stone!

He walked unsteadily towards the statue of Finlay. 'Fin,' he whispered helplessly. He felt dizzy with shock.

What was he going to do? What were Finlay's mum and dad going to say?

He looked into Finlay's grey face. With a gasp he jumped back. Finlay's eyes were still normal!

'What-what . . .' he stammered as Finlay looked at him frantically, his eyes darting from side to side. 'You're not dead!' Max exclaimed, relief hitting him like a sledgehammer.

Finlay couldn't say anything – he couldn't speak or move.

Max's thoughts whirled. He touched Finlay's arm but it was as cold and hard as a stone pillar. Finlay might not be dead but he really *had* turned to stone! *What am I going to do?* Max thought. *Help!*

A savage snarl rang out.

Max's gaze flew to the grassy square. The dog was lifting its heads from the floor. Its six burning eyes fixed on him and an even louder, more vicious growl ripped through the silence.

*Silence!*

Max's heart sank.

The batteries of the keyboard must have finally run out.

Barking furiously, Cerberus leapt to his feet and charged towards Max and the stone statue of Finlay.

Max leapt back just in time. The beast was pulled up short just in front of Finlay. One set of jaws crashed closed around Finlay's leg. As its teeth met the rock-hard surface, the dog howled in pain. Its sleep didn't seem to have done anything to improve its temper.

Max ran forward. Finlay might be stone, but he wasn't going to let Cerberus savage him. 'Get away from Fin! Get back!' he yelled, picking up some bricks from the ground and chucking them as hard as he could at the beast. His throws fell short. Cerberus raced at the bricks, grabbing them in his mouth and crunching them up as if Max was throwing bones for him. Finally one made contact with one of his heads. He lunged furiously at Max.

There was a grating sound of metal on stone and one of the rings pulled free from the plinth. Max gasped in alarm. The two remaining rings holding the dog creaked alarmingly. If they gave way too then Cerberus would be free . . .

Max raced back to the shed for safety. What was he going to do? Fin was turned to stone. Cerberus was about to break his chains. There was no one to help.

Hercules' voice suddenly seemed to echo in Max ear. *Remember, even if all seems lost there will always be a way out if you look hard enough.*

*I'm looking*, thought Max desperately. *I'm looking really hard!*

His eyes fell on a piece of paper on the floor. The riddle! He'd dropped it when Finlay had turned to stone. He picked it up.

If only Fin had listened to him and not grabbed the earth apple. The riddle had said that the element to leave stood alone and was in the grassy square. Well, fire, water and air couldn't stand anywhere – but things of stone did, and the stone statue of Cerberus had stood in the grassy square. The one they had to leave was

earth − *stone which comes from earth*;
the rest of the riddle had just been
a trick to distract them, like he'd
thought.

He looked at the riddle. A line
suddenly seemed to jump out at him:
*If you choose wrongly, mark these words . . .*

Max's breath caught in his throat.
Finlay *had* chosen wrongly. Maybe the
riddle would tell him what to do to
turn Finlay back!

'*If you choose wrongly, mark these words,*'
he read out. '*Two elements may break a
third. The water from the cherub's breath,
can split the stone and save from death.*'

Max glanced out of the shed towards
the bronze statue of the cherub. As he
looked at the cherub's trumpet, his eyes
suddenly widened. The trumpet! The

cherub was blowing out through it!
Maybe '*water from the cherub's breath*'
meant the water that came out of the
trumpet when the trick fountain was
triggered.

Suddenly everything seemed to click
into place in his brain. If he could get
the fountain to spray on Finlay then
maybe the magic would be reversed.
The only problem was how did he start
the fountain? He ran to the door of the
shed.

Cerberus was hurling his weight
against the two remaining chains,
desperate to tear the flesh from Max's
bones. With a grating crunch the
second ring gave way.

Now there was just one chain and
ring holding the beast! Fear flooded

through Max. How soon before that
gave way too . . .

*I have to get that fountain spouting,* he
thought frantically. But there was no
way he could get past the dog to the
flagstones. If only there was someone
else to help him. But it was just him
and the dog . . .

The dog!

An idea exploded into Max's mind.
Suddenly remembering how Cerberus
had chased after the bricks he'd
chucked at him, he grabbed a brick
from the floor and threw it towards the
flagstones. It fell short, but with a snarl
Cerberus chased after it and grabbed it
in his teeth.

Max grabbed another brick. This time
his arm snapped back and he let the

brick go with all the strength he could muster. The brick sailed through the air and landed right on the third flagstone.

The dog leapt straight on to the flagstone after it. The second its weight hit the stone, a jet of water shot straight up into the air. It started raining down on the grassy square. It fell on the dog and the grass – and Fin!

*Crack!*

Max's heart leapt. Splits started spreading from the top of Fin's head and his fingers, spreading all the way to his toes. It was as if the stone was ice and starting to thaw, revealing the person inside. Finlay was turning back to normal!

'Fin!' Max yelled in delight.

Cerberus stared at the cracking statue of Finlay. The hackles rose on the back of his neck and he growled in fury. He jumped off the flagstone and the fountain immediately stopped. Barking

angrily, Cerberus threw himself towards the boys, his massive paws clawing the ground, his powerful muscles straining, his burning eyes filled with hatred and hunger. With a shock, Max saw the last remaining ring tear out of the ground. Cerberus was free!

The beast threw back its three heads and gave a bloodcurdling howl of triumph. Then it charged straight at Max **and the** half-stone figure of Finlay – its deadly jaws wide open.

# CHAPTER EIGHT

## PETRIFIED!

Cerberus bore down on Max and
Finlay, his different heads barking,
growling and spraying drool.

'We're going to die!' Max yelled in
horror.

'No, we're not!' Finlay said, his voice
strangely hollow as he shouted through
stone lips that were gradually turning
back to normal. And as the slavering

beast powered towards them, Finlay
lifted his hand that was slowly turning
back to flesh and chucked the glittering
apple away from him and straight into
the nearest of the dog's mouths.

A crack snapped through the air like gunshot. The dog's teeth snapped shut on the apple and stayed shut. Grey stone started to spread across its face. Thick ropes of drool hanging from its jaw hardened like icicles. The other two heads howled in surprise. But they didn't howl for long. Within seconds the hard stone was engulfing the dog, turning it to a statue where it stood. Its howl became a whimper – then it broke off with a strangled sound and there was silence.

'One stands alone,' Max breathed, staring at the statue in front of them. He swung round. The last of the grey stone was just disappearing from Finlay's hair. 'Cool or what? That was a brilliant idea, Fin!'

Finlay grinned. 'Just call me a genius!'
He looked at the dog's eyes, which still
burned furiously in the stone even
though it couldn't move. 'Don't think
he'll be winning Best Freaky Mythical
Killer at Crufts any time soon!'

'He looks really mad!' Max said,
sounding very satisfied.

'Guess we'd better not tread on the
trick flagstone, then,' Finlay commented.
He rubbed his knee. It was bleeding
where the dog had snapped at his
stone skin.

'Are you OK?' Max asked.

'Yeah,' Finlay admitted. 'I'm glad I was
turned to stone though. If I hadn't been
a statue at the time, I wouldn't have a
leg to stand on now! Ha!'

Max grinned at Fin's rubbish joke.

'So what did it feel like to be stone?'

'Weird,' Finlay replied. 'Like I couldn't feel anything with my body but my brain was still working. And the worst thing was I thought I was going to have to stay like that forever.' He shuddered for a moment. 'Thanks for working out how to save me.'

'S'OK,' Max said. 'I remembered what Hercules said about there always being a way out and found the answer in the riddle.'

'It's lucky it wasn't the other way round and that it wasn't you who was turned to stone, Max,' Finlay said. 'I'd never have worked out what to do. But then I guess you wouldn't have grabbed the apple like I did.' He looked a bit ashamed of himself. 'I just wasn't afraid of anything. Not even of being wrong. Hercules was right; having extra courage has made me act dumb.'

Max grinned at him. 'It doesn't matter. Least we can take the apples back to Juno now.'

Finlay's eyes lit up. 'Yeah. We've done the task, haven't we?' He pulled the wind and water apples out of his pockets. 'Come on, let's get the last apple. The sooner we get back to the castle with the apples, the sooner Juno's magic will go and Cerberus will turn back into a proper statue.' They ran back to the shed and Max took the fire apple off the pedestal.

'The Three Golden Apples!' he said, holding up the final apple. 'We've got them all!'

'Let's go!' Finlay exclaimed.

'I wonder if Cerberus will stay
where he is when Juno's magic goes
and he turns completely back to stone,'

Max said as they left the shed and hurried past where Cerberus stood. 'And if he does, what the owners will say. And about the fact that half their garden wall's been knocked down!'

'It's all right.' Finlay grinned. 'With any luck, they'll blame it on the Brownies running wild!'

'That reminds me, I'd better put their keyboard back,' Max said. 'You coming?'

'Just a sec,' said Finlay. He picked up a fallen stick, ran back to Cerberus and held it up to each of his stone snouts. 'Here we are, boy. Fetch!' He threw the stick, and smiled. 'Oh, I forgot – you can't, can you?' He tickled the nearest muzzle. 'Sorry about that!'

Laughing together, he and Max raced out of the walled garden and down the path.

'Three apples!' Finlay yelled to the sky as they scrambled into the castle keep a little while later. 'We've got them, Juno! Come and see for yourself!'

'Fin!' Max protested in alarm.

'Who cares if she comes?' Finlay threw the apples triumphantly into the air.

There was a thunderclap and the apples vanished.

Finlay felt a swirling in his chest and the next second a golden light was streaming from him as the superpower of courage flooded out. It swept across the courtyard to the tower and hit the back wall. Suddenly Finlay didn't feel quite so brave about facing Juno. There was the sound of crumbling, breaking stones as Hercules' face appeared, but the noise was drowned out by a second thunderclap.

Juno suddenly stood in the castle keep, her cloak billowing round her, her face dark with rage.

'You succeeded!' she exclaimed.

Finlay backed away to join Max. 'Y-yes,' he said, looking into the goddess's terrifying face, his extra courage now gone.

'You got past Cerberus and solved the riddle!' Juno hissed.

Hercules' voice rang out. '*Cerberus!*'

The goddess swung round. 'Yes, Cerberus. I placed him there to guard the apples!'

'That is not playing by the rules, Juno!' Hercules exclaimed. 'Fighting Cerberus is a task in itself. It was one of my tasks when I completed my twelve labours. It is not fair to expect the boys to get past him *and* fetch the apples!' He turned to the boys. 'To have subdued Cerberus and brought back the three golden apples is an astonishing achievement. You must *both* have shown great courage today – and wisdom. Courage on its own would not have been enough.' He turned back to Juno. 'You have made the boys complete two tasks for the reward of freeing one superpower!'

Juno twirled a lock of her hair. 'I never said they *had* to fight Cerberus. The task was getting the apples.' She grinned evilly. 'They just had to get past him to be able to do it.'

'That's cheating, Juno!' Hercules said furiously.

'Not by my rules.' Juno clicked her fingers. Hercules' mouth continued to open and close but no words came out. 'And *my* rules are the ones that count, Hercules,' Juno breathed triumphantly.

Hercules looked as if he was about to explode with rage. Ignoring him, Juno turned to the boys. Her voice turned icy cold. 'Do not think you have won yet. There is one more task to complete and tomorrow you *will* die!'

Finlay felt a shiver of fear run down his spine but no way was he going to show Juno how scared he felt. 'We won't!' he told her defiantly. 'We'll do whatever task you set us. We'll get Hercules his last superpower back.'

'Yeah!' Max nodded. 'Then he'll be able to break free from the tower!'

'Never!' Juno shrieked and with a clap of her hands, she disappeared in a flash of lightning. At the same time, the stones around Hercules' face closed over and he disappeared.

The boys stood in the suddenly silent castle.

'Juno seemed really mad with us,' Max said slowly.

'Yeah,' Finlay agreed. He forced a grin. '*Barking* mad if you ask me!'

Max took a deep breath. 'Well, it doesn't matter what she says, we'll complete the task tomorrow and free Hercules.'

Finlay nodded. 'Even if we have to fight ten more of those Cerberus dogs!'

Max frowned. 'You sure you haven't still got some of that super-courage inside you?'

'You mean you *wouldn't* fight two Cerberuses tomorrow?' Finlay said.

Max didn't answer.

'Bet you would,' Finlay went on. 'You did all sorts of brave stuff today and you didn't even have the extra courage. You stopped the dog biting me when I was stone, you got the keyboard, you made the dog jump on the fountain flagstone *and* you solved the riddle. We'd never have got the apples without you.'

'Or you,' Max told him. 'You were the one doing the Lara Croft stuff to get to the apples in the first place and you stopped the dog at the end when it was about to eat us.'

They looked at each other.

'Guess we did it together,' Finlay said.

'And we will again tomorrow,' Max put in determinedly. 'We'll beat Juno and get Hercules his last superpower back.'

Finlay nodded and put his hand up in the air. Max met it in a high five.

'Tomorrow!' they both yelled.

# ABOUT THE AUTHOR

ALEX CLIFF LIVES IN A VILLAGE IN LEICESTERSHIRE, NEXT DOOR TO FIN AND JUST DOWN THE ROAD FROM MAX, BUT UNFORTUNATELY THERE IS NO CASTLE ON THE OUTSKIRTS OF THE VILLAGE. ALEX'S HOME IS FILLED WITH TWO CHILDREN AND TWO LARGE AND VERY SLOBBERY PET MONSTERS.

# WILL MAX AND FIN SAVE HERCULES IN TIME?

# HOW WILL THEY FACE A HERD OF STAMPEDING BEASTS?

## DID YOU KNOW?

Hercules lived in Ancient Greece. He was the son of a woman named Alcmene and the god Zeus. When Hercules was a baby he could fight snakes with his bare hands! The labours he had to complete were originally set for him by his cousin Eurystheus, King of Mycenae.

### CERBERUS

Cerberus is one of the most famous monsters in ancient myth. He was the howling three-headed dog who guarded the gates to Hades, the underworld. Hercules wrestled him and dragged him back in chains to Eurystheus, who was so scared that he jumped into a bronze jar!

# CAN MAX AND FIN DEFEAT MAN-EATING BIRDS?

## DID YOU KNOW?

Hercules lived in Ancient Greece. He was the son of a woman named Alcmene and the god Zeus. When Hercules was a baby he could fight snakes with his bare hands! The labours he had to complete were originally set for him by his cousin Eurystheus, King of Mycenae.

### THE ERYMANTHIAN BOAR

This was a ferocious beast that attacked people and destroyed everything in its path. When Hercules first fought it he had to look for it on the Mountain of Erymanthus and chase it from its hiding place. Unlike some of his other labours, he had to capture this beast alive and take it to Mycenae in chains.

puffin.co.uk

# YOUR
# SUPER POWERS
## QUEST

## YOU NEED:
2 players
2 counters
1 dice
and nerves of steel!

## YOU MUST:
Collect all **seven** superpowers
and save Hercules, who has
been trapped in the castle by
the evil goddess, Juno. All you
have to do is roll the dice and
follow the steps on the books
– try not to land on Juno's rock
or one of the monsters!

## YOU CAN:
### PLAY BOOK BY BOOK
The game is only complete when all seven books in the series are lined
up. But if you don't have them all yet, you can still complete the quests!
Whoever lands on the 'GO' rock first is the winner of that particular quest.

### PLAY THE WHOLE GAME
Whoever collects all seven superpowers and is first to land on the final
rock has completed the entire quest and saved Hercules!

## REMEMBER:
If you land on a 'Back to the Start' symbol, don't worry – you don't have
to go all the way back to book one – just back to the start of the game
on the book you are playing.

# GOOD LUCK, SUPERHEROES!